Whoa! Blue Betty!

Text copyright © 2021 by Hayley Cronin

Illustrations copyright © 2021 by Deborah Cronin

ISBN 978-1-66782-016-3

All rights reserved.

*For my grandma, the writer,
and to Brett, Berkeley and Hayden, the inspiration. -HC*

*For Betty Wilson, who insisted that I had artistic talent
despite my futile ventures into ballet and ukulele. -DC*

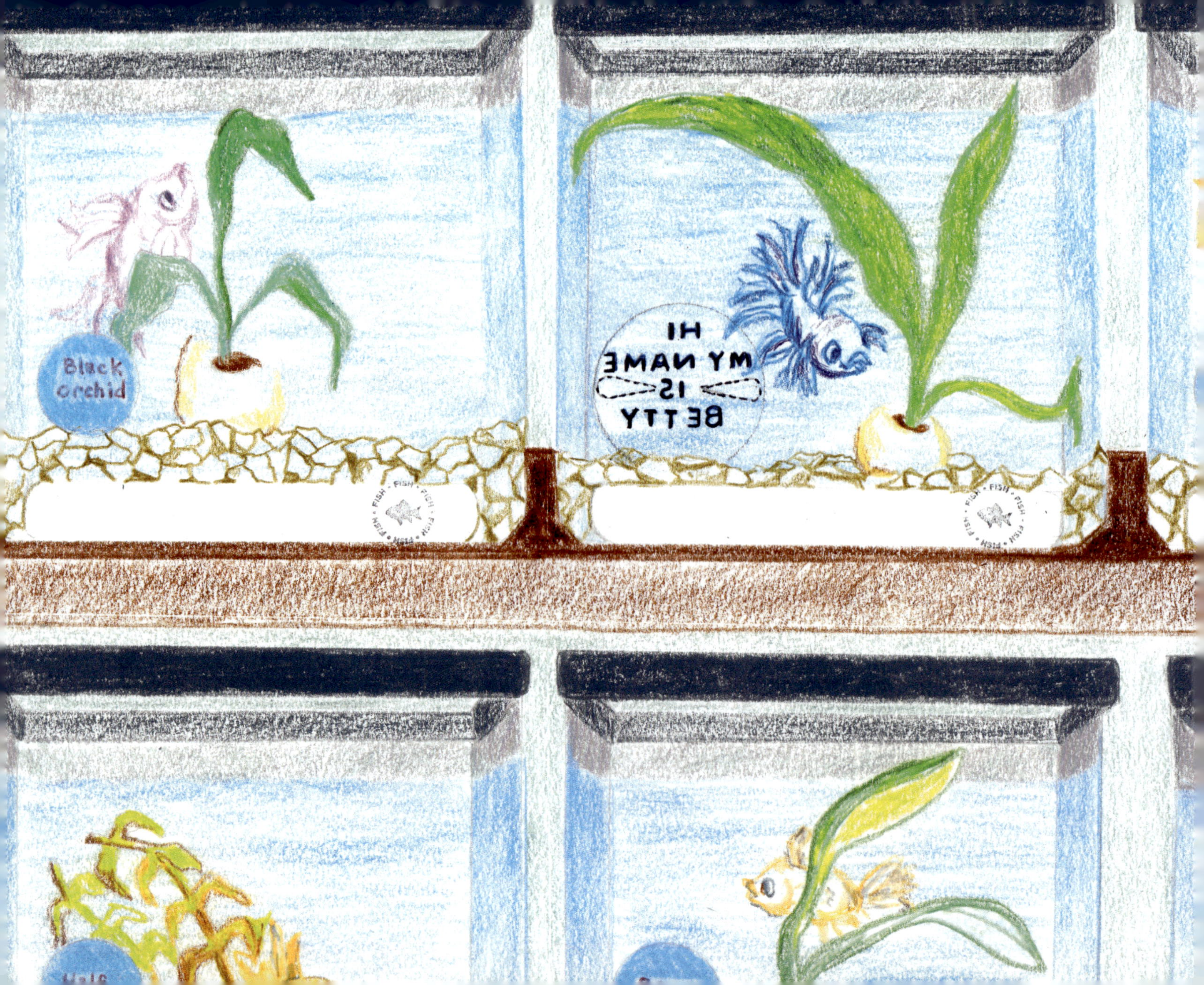
Black orchid
HI
MY NAME
IS
BETTY

BETTY was a Betta,
blue and shining on the shelf.
But despite her STRIKING colors,
she chose to hide herself.

Hiding behind a plant
started when she was a tiny fish.
She was timid, shy and quite unsure
there was anyone
to hear her WISH.

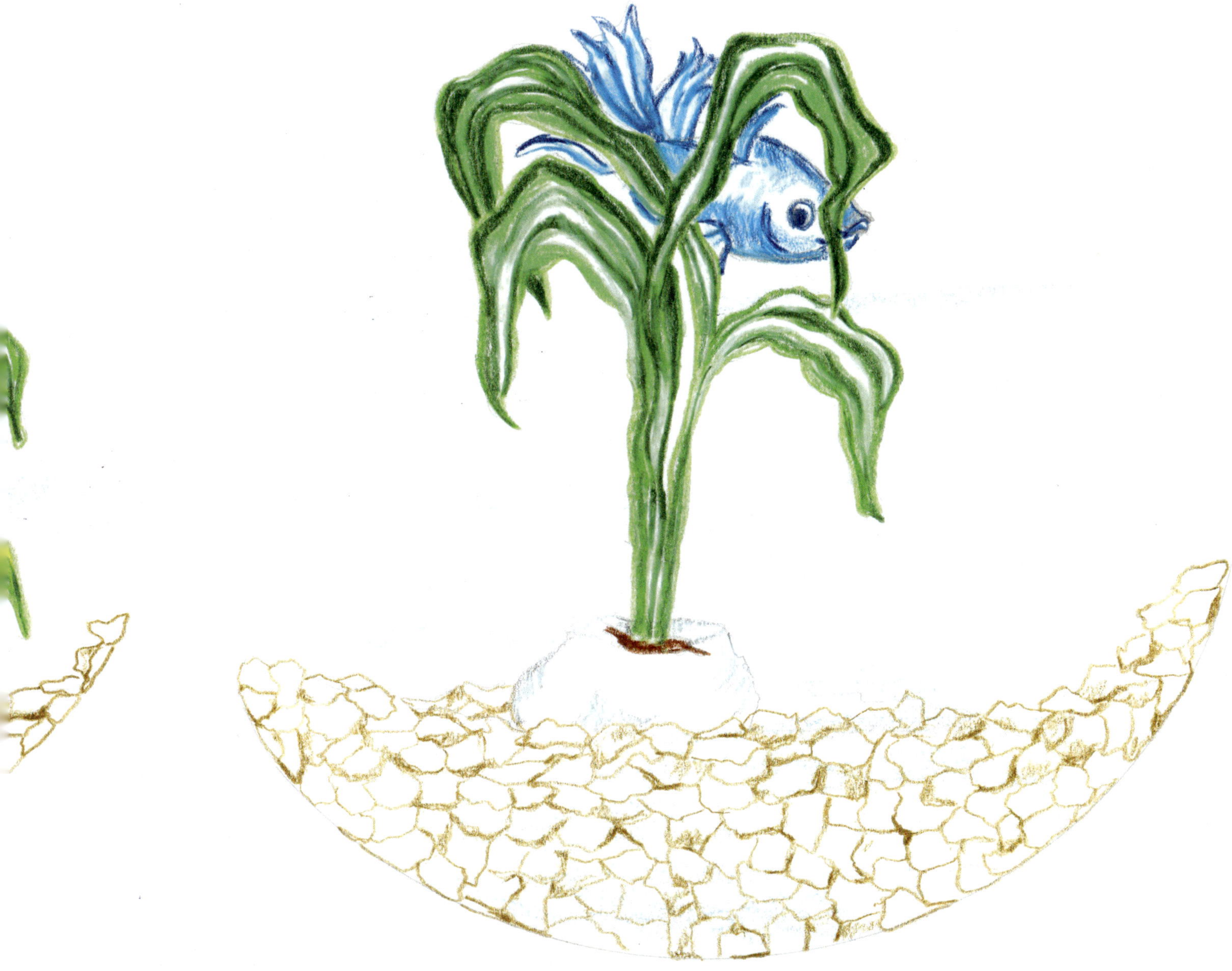

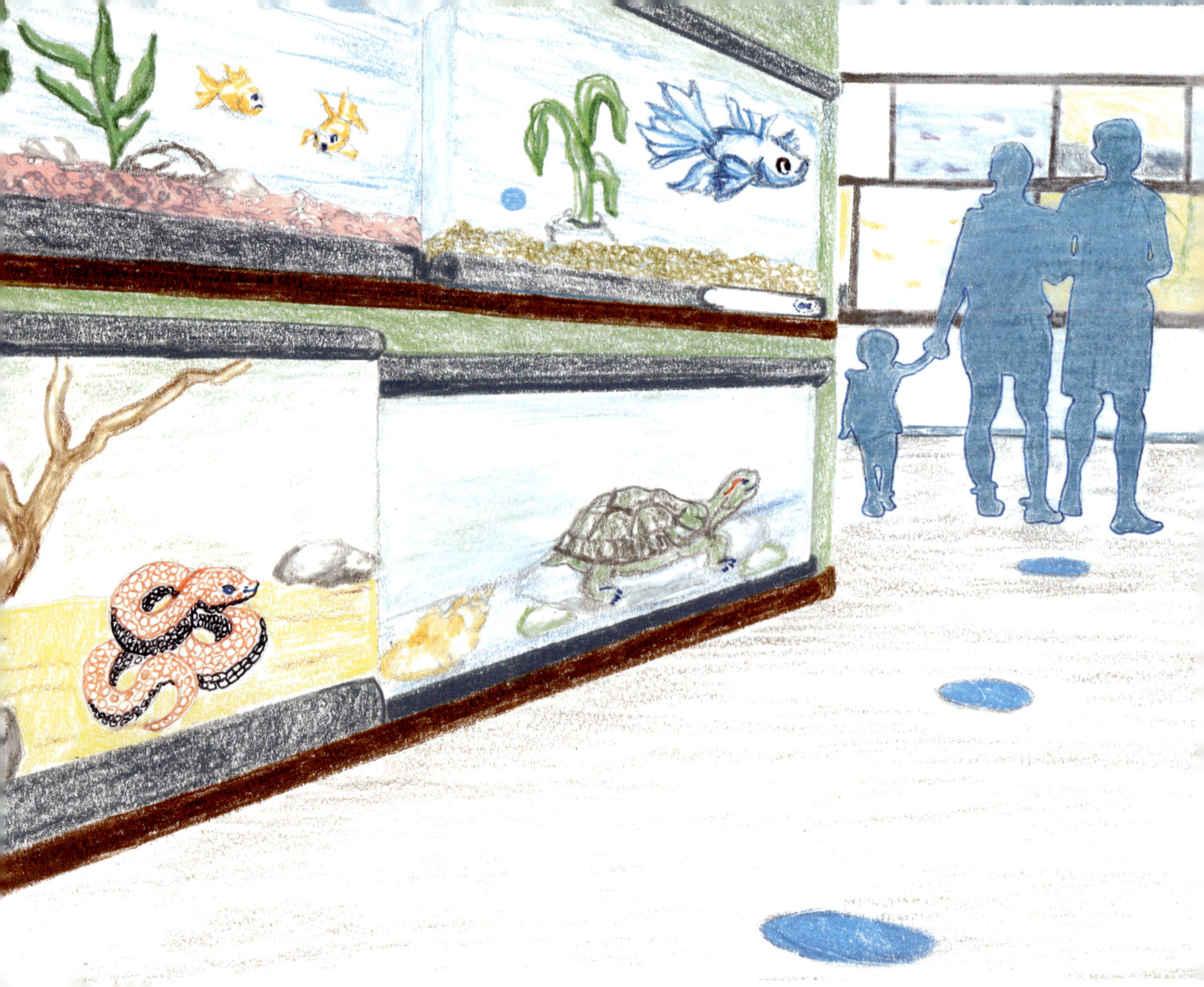

"WHOA! BLUE BETTY!"
she dreamed they'd say.
"Gliding around your tank so free
with your shimmering blue and purple fins,
I'm so HAPPY you belong to me!"

All day long she swam and dreamt
of the PERFECT life to be.
Something beyond her tiny tank,
with a loving FAMILY.

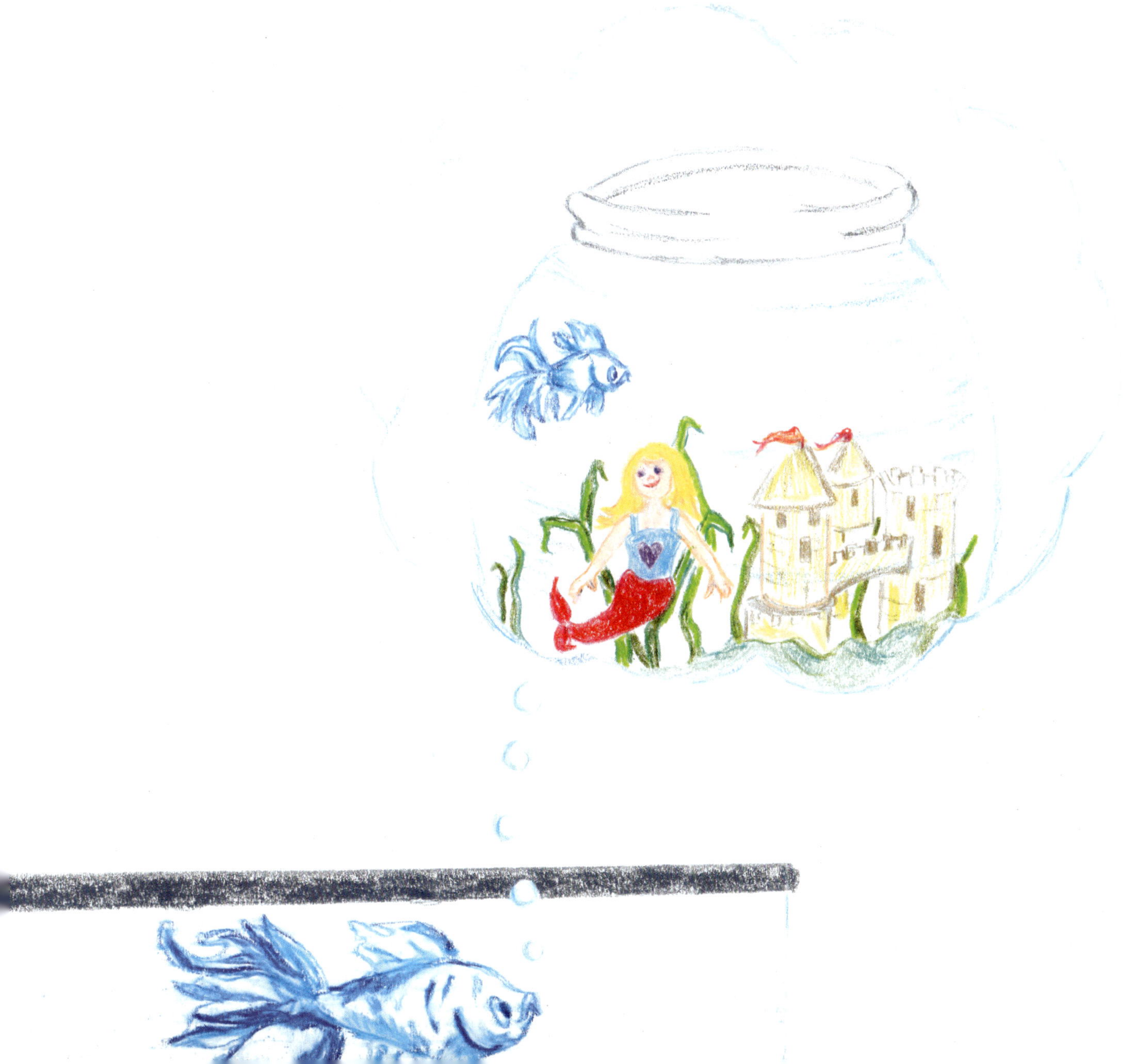

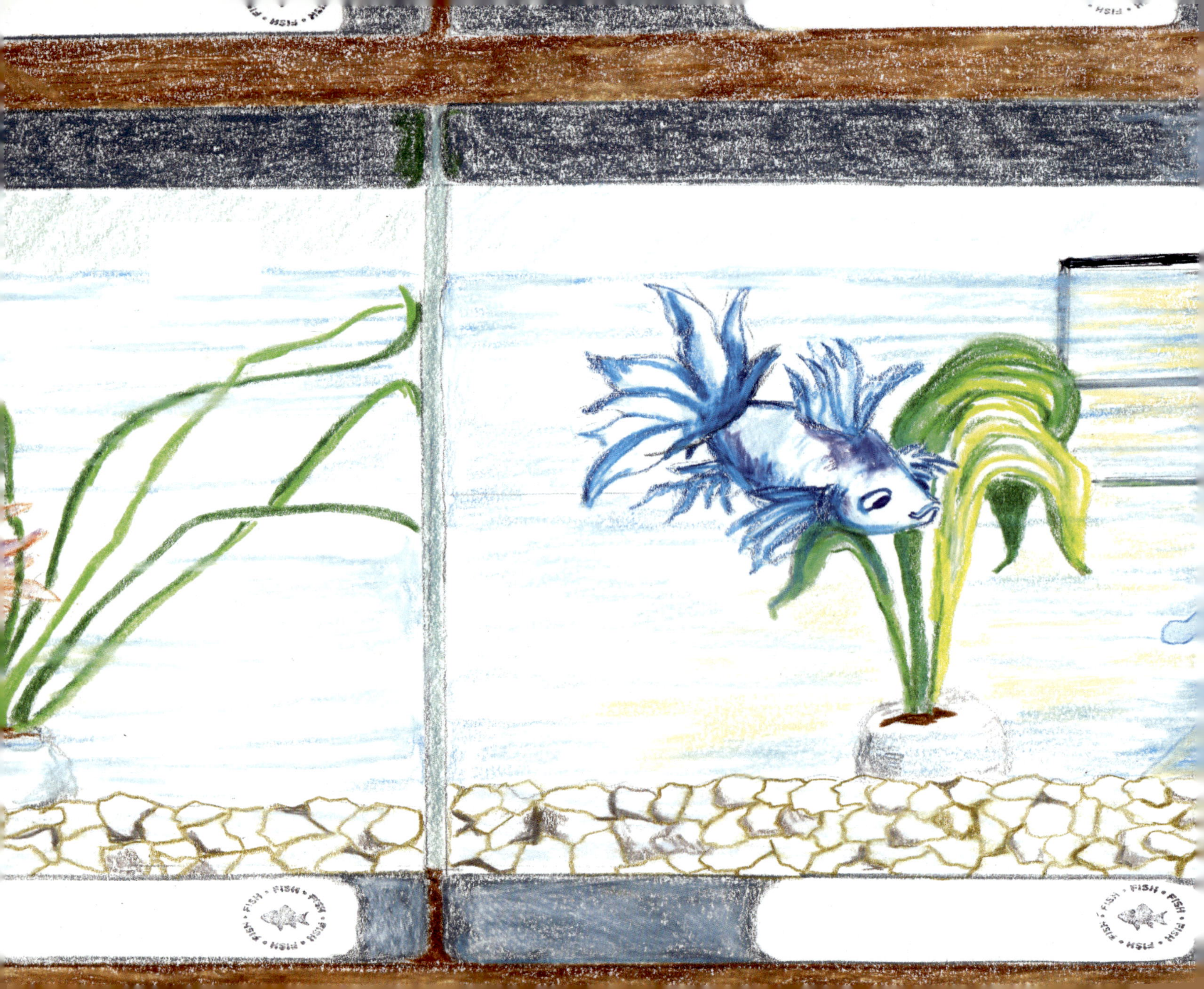
FISH • FISH • FISH
FISH • FISH • FISH

Just then a family appeared,
and with it a tiny girl.
BETTY took cover behind her plant
and observed the outside world.

Then Betty noticed something, something so SIMILAR it was classic. While she was hidden behind a plant, the GIRL cowered behind a basket.

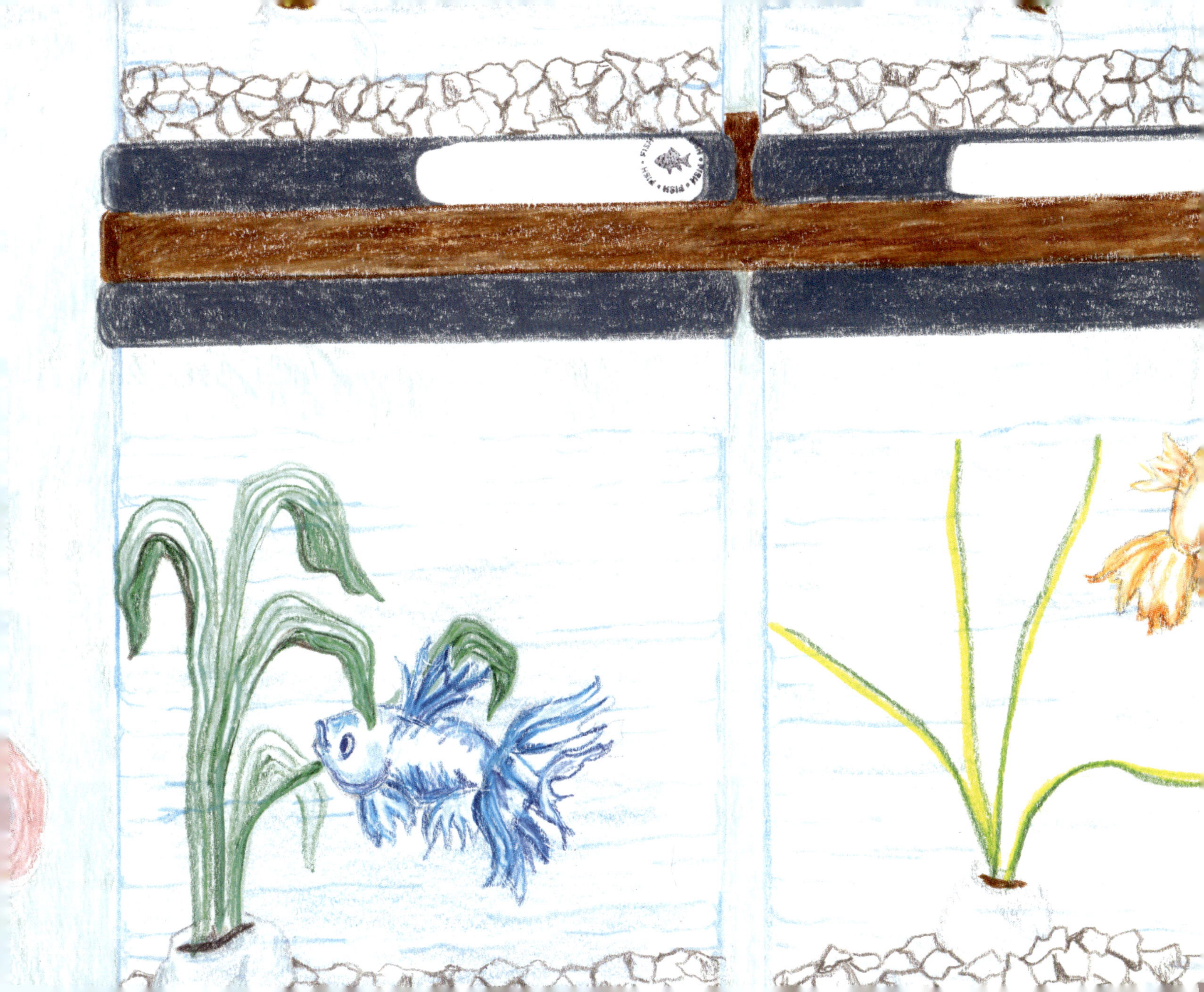
FISH • FISH • FISH • FISH •

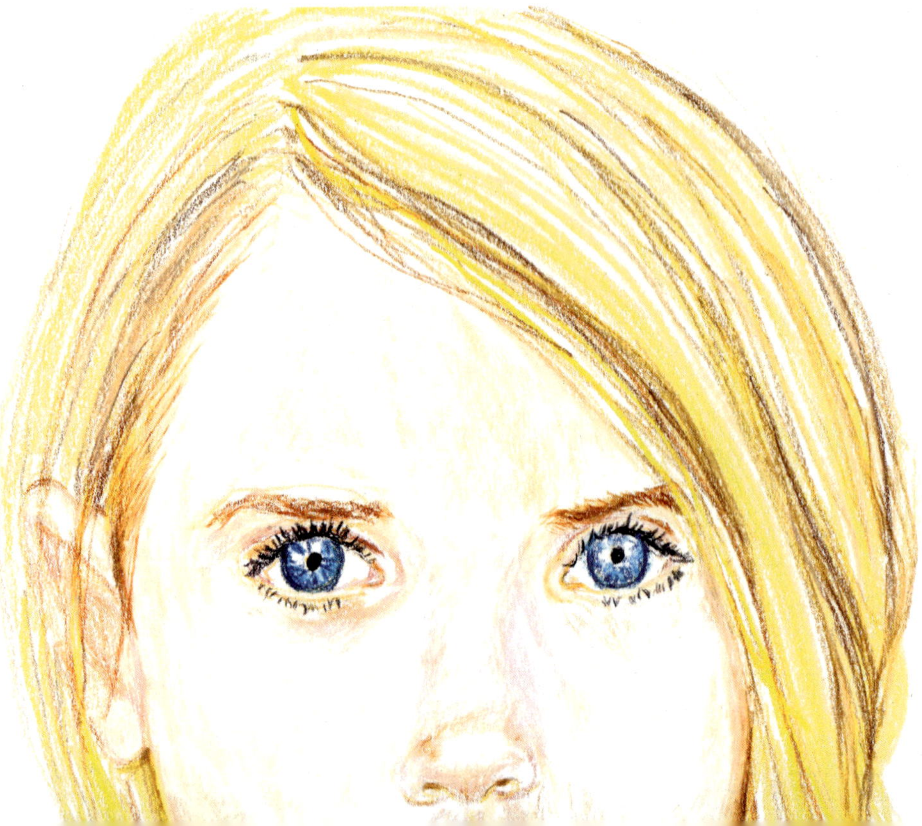

The girl's name was BERKIE.
She was bashful, blonde and bright.
Her eyes, a similar SPARKLING blue,
were fixed on Betty,
while she held her mom so tight.

"WHOA! BLUE BERKIE!"
Betty wanted to shout,
"standing so close to me.
I'm coy and quiet
just like YOU.
Are we really meant
to be?"

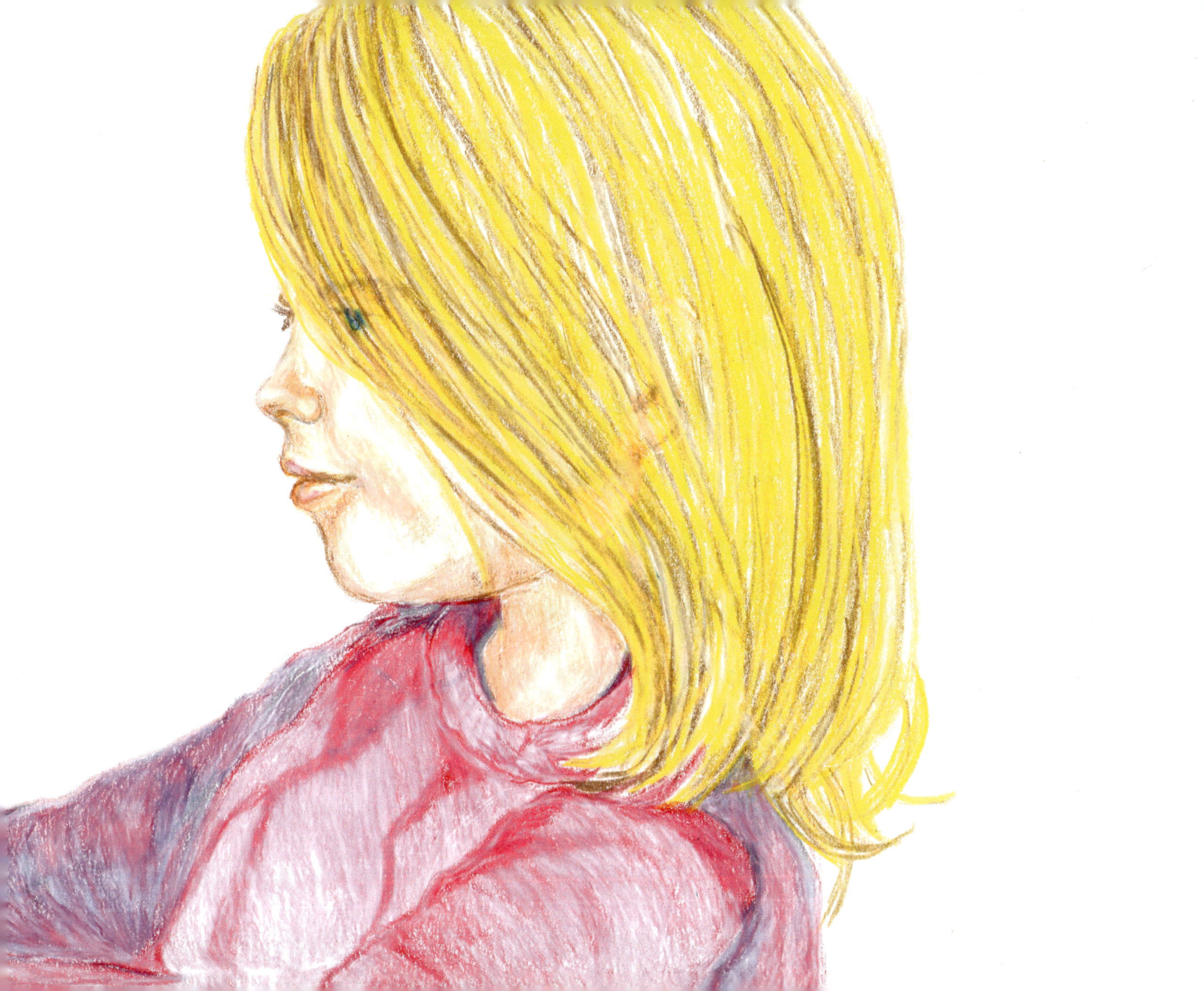

"Being shy and out of sight
could be our SUPERPOWER.
Side by side, we'd shine so bright–
best friends at any hour."

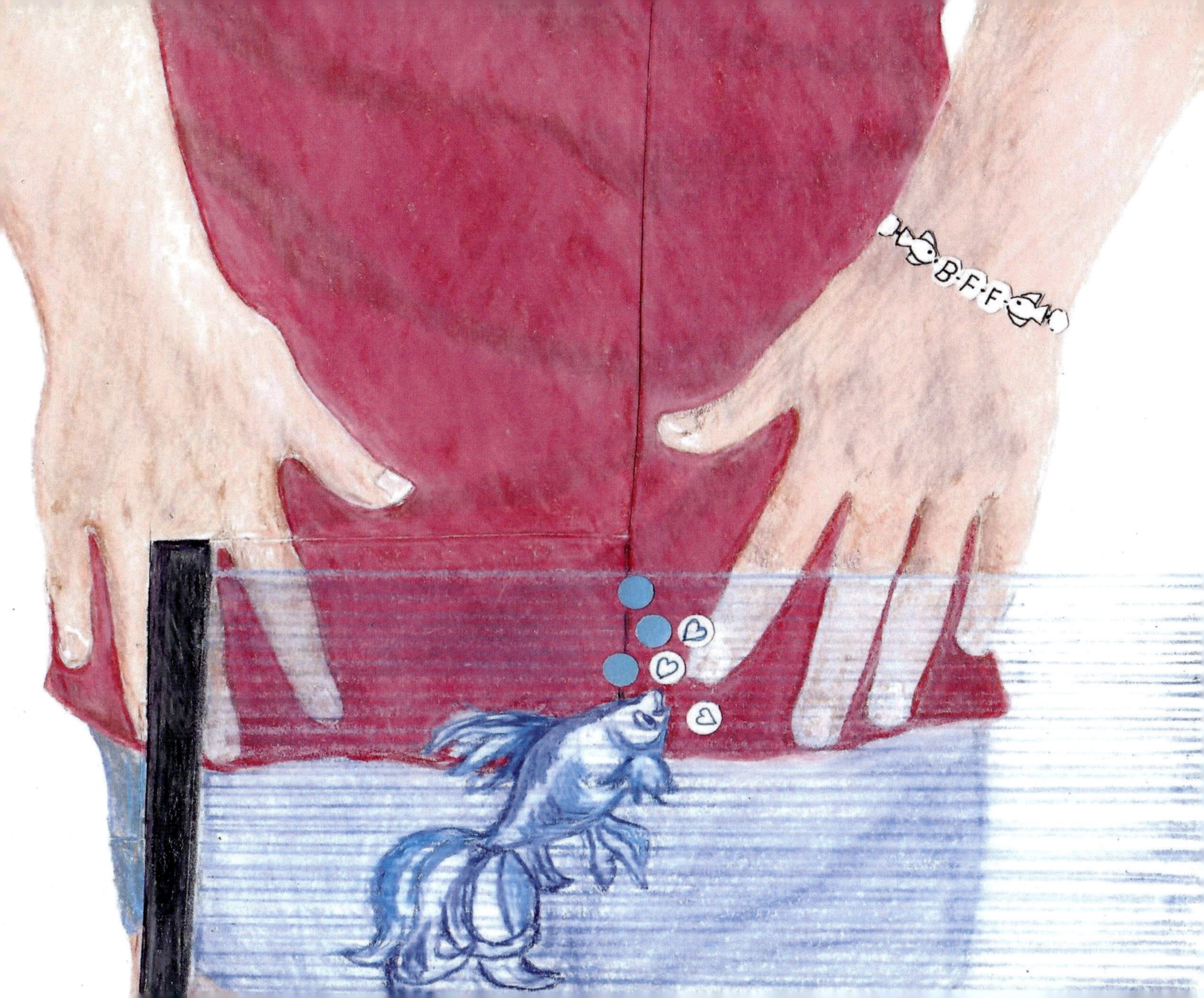
B·F·F

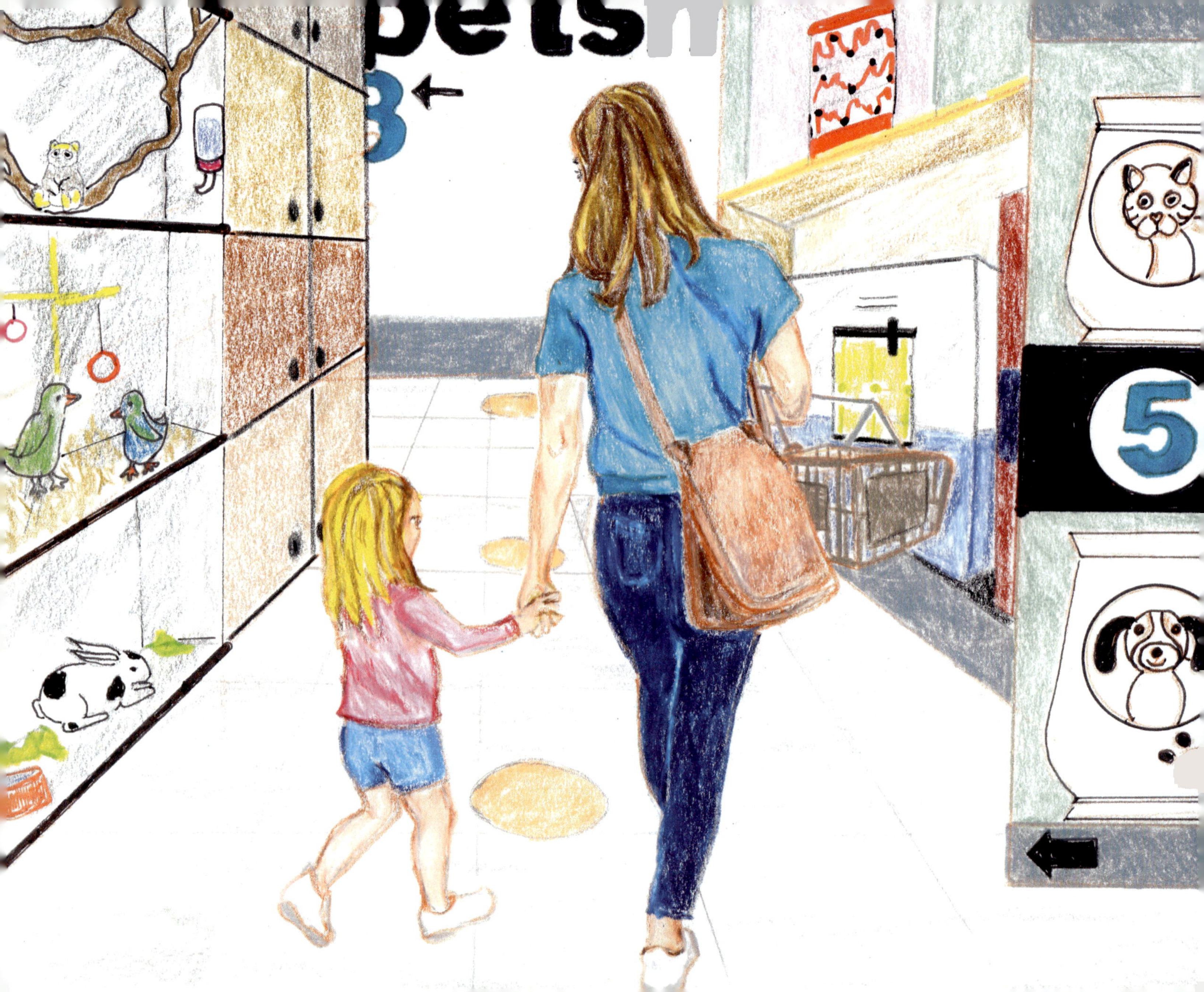
pets
8
5

But Berkie's mom had other plans,
and together they walked AWAY.
Both Betty and Berkie considered
maybe TODAY just wasn't their day.

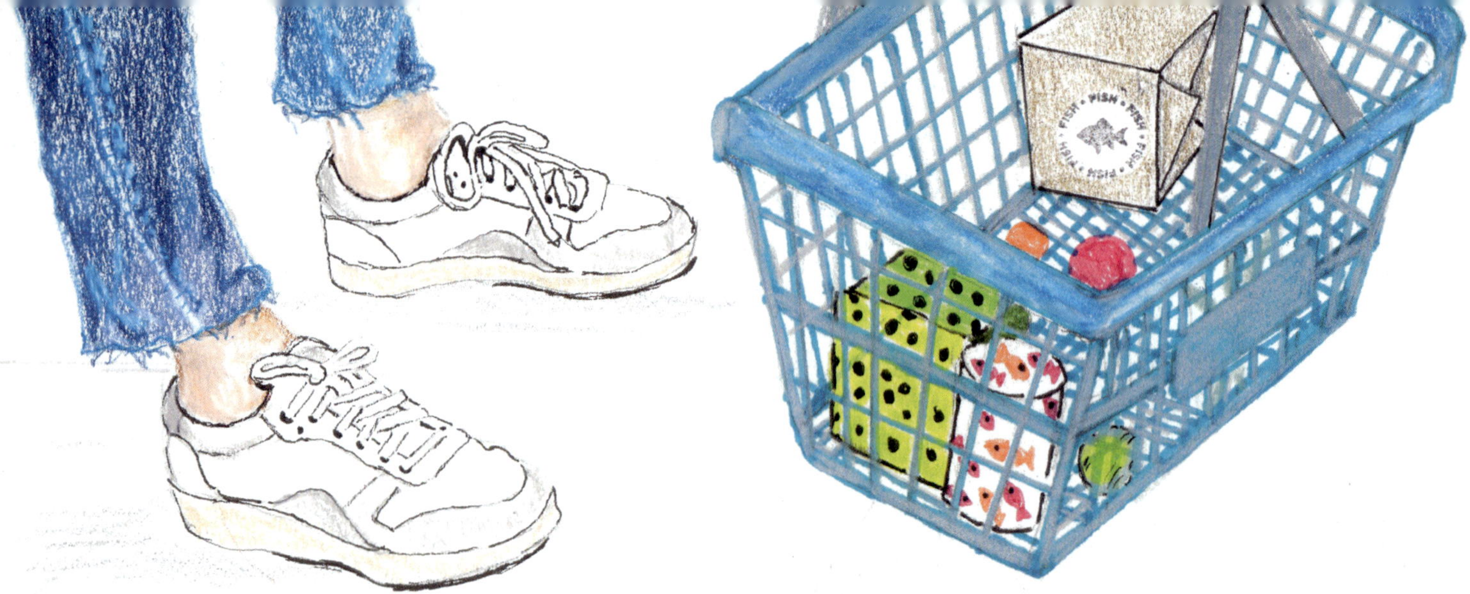
FISH

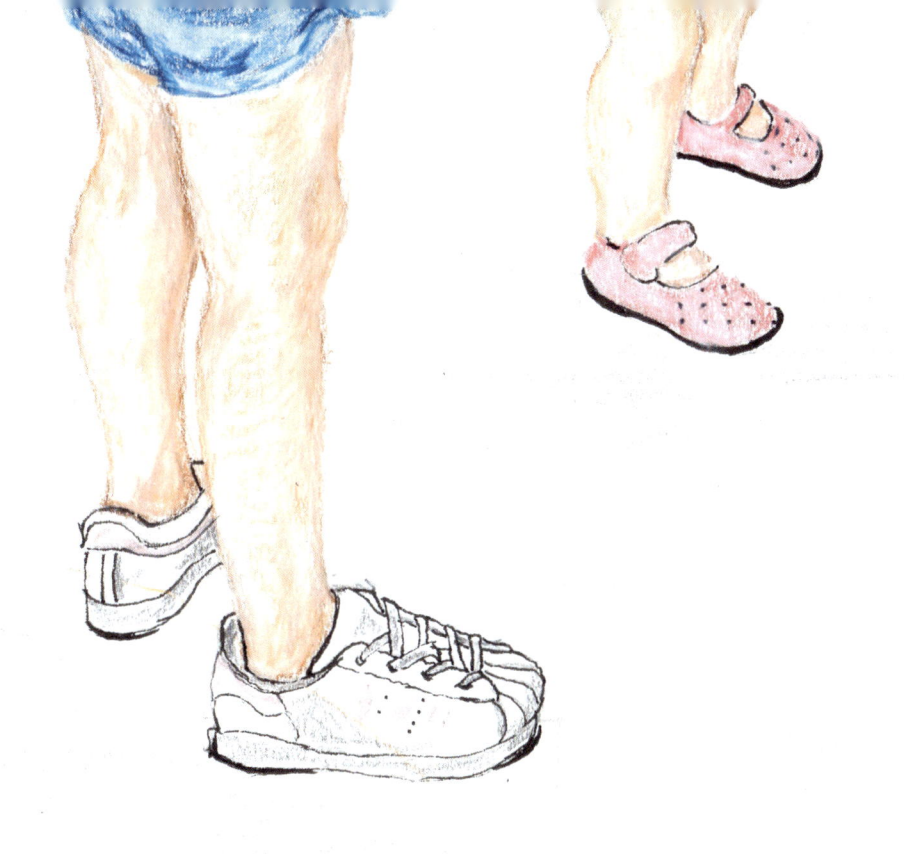

Not far down the aisle,
BETTY watched them browse.
She was heartbroken, helpless,
and really very DOWN.

"OH! BLUE BETTY!"
she muttered to herself.
"Gliding around your tank so free
with these shimmering blue and purple fins,
one day they'll NOTICE me."

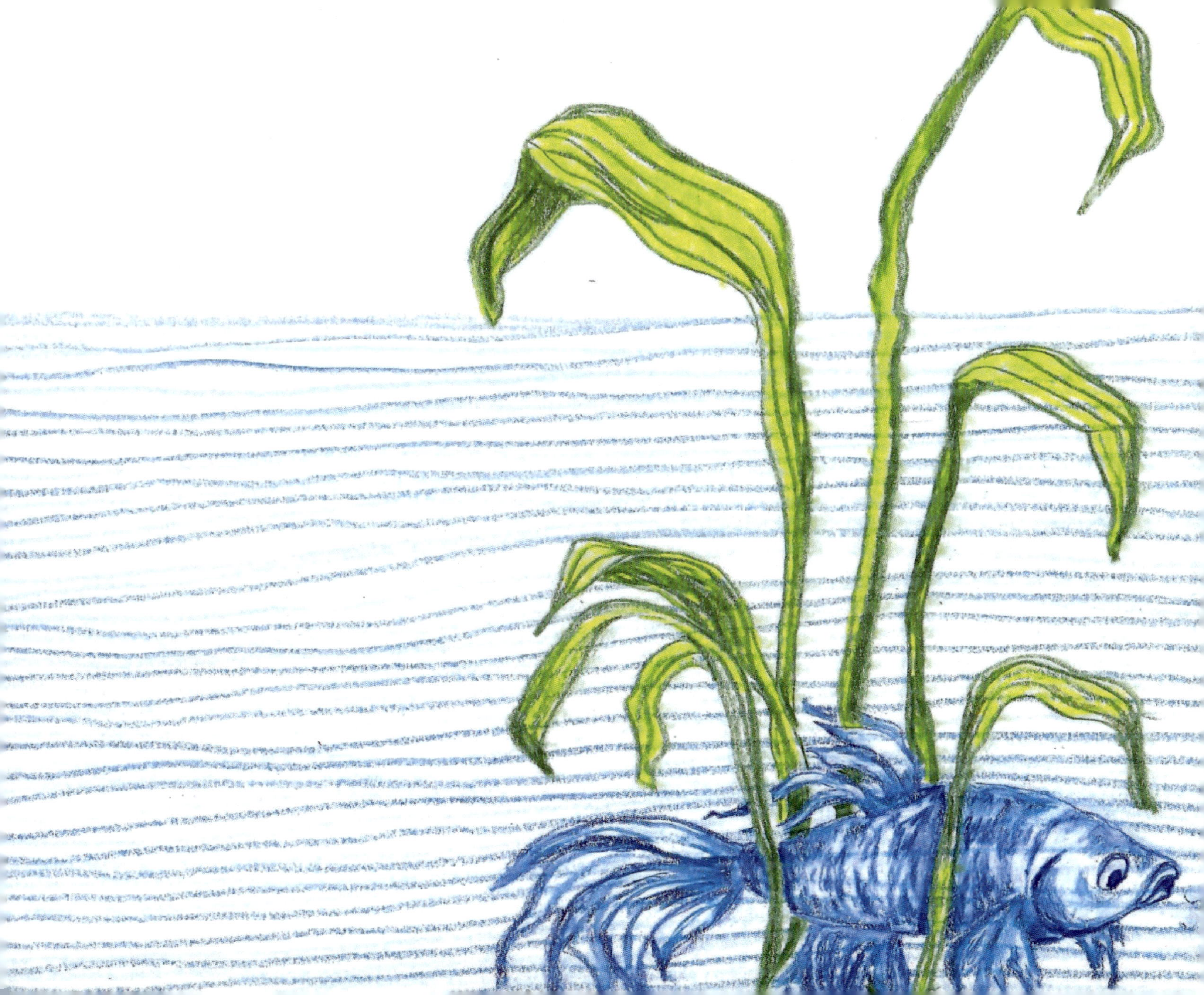

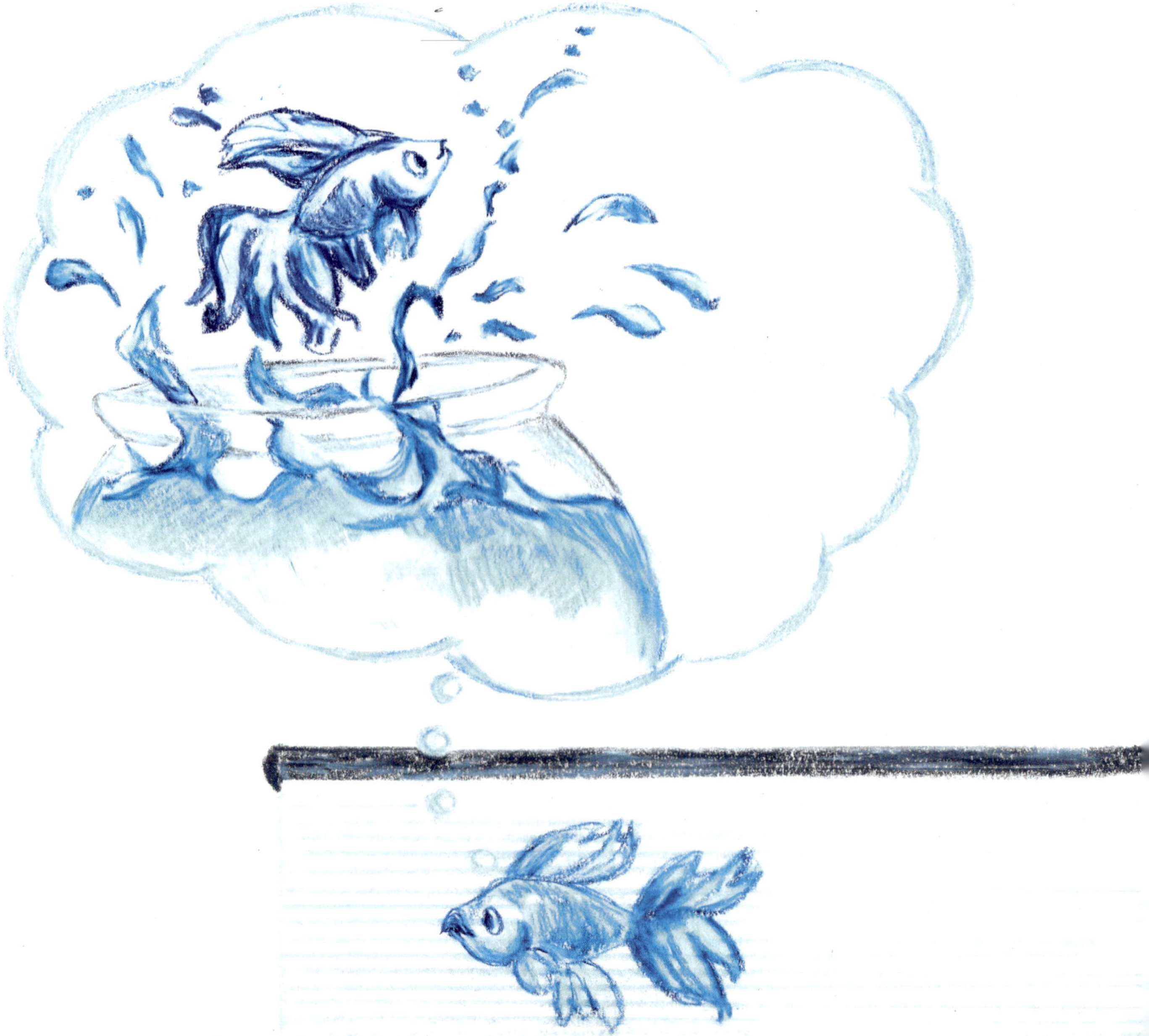

"If only my feelings matched my fins,
I'd be STRIKING, strong, and loud.
No longer hidden behind a plant,
I would make a family PROUD."

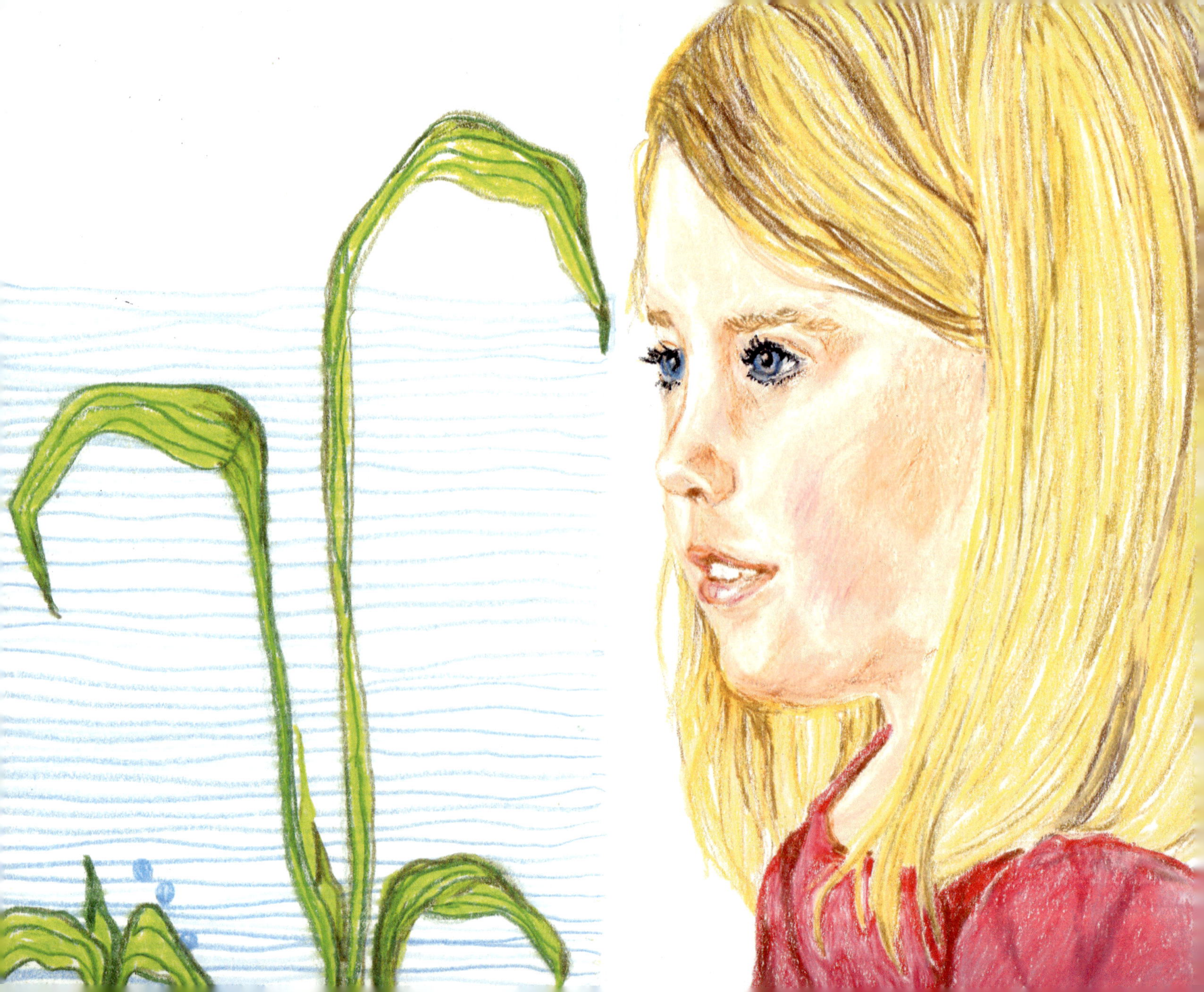

While she was wallowing in her tank,
Betty missed the BIG surprise.
When she looked up, staring back at her
were BERKIE'S big blue eyes!

Betty noticed Berkie's tug and point
and a basket FULL of supplies.
Berkie reached for Betty's tank—
this was happening before her EYES!

6 fish

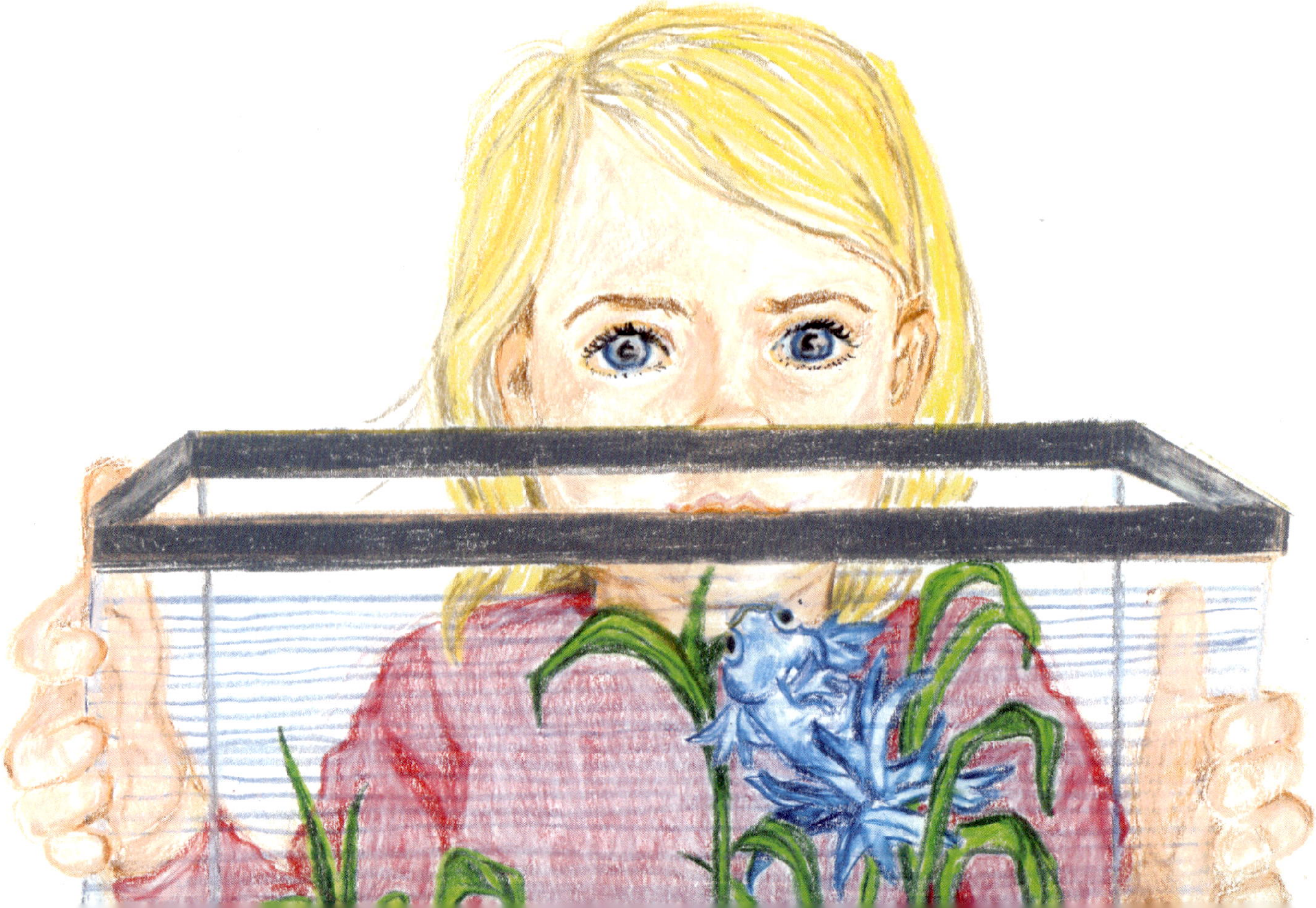

Flowing fins, Betty emerged
from behind her plant,
to ADMIRE the sight before her.
The tiny girl, now standing TALL,
proudly became her owner.

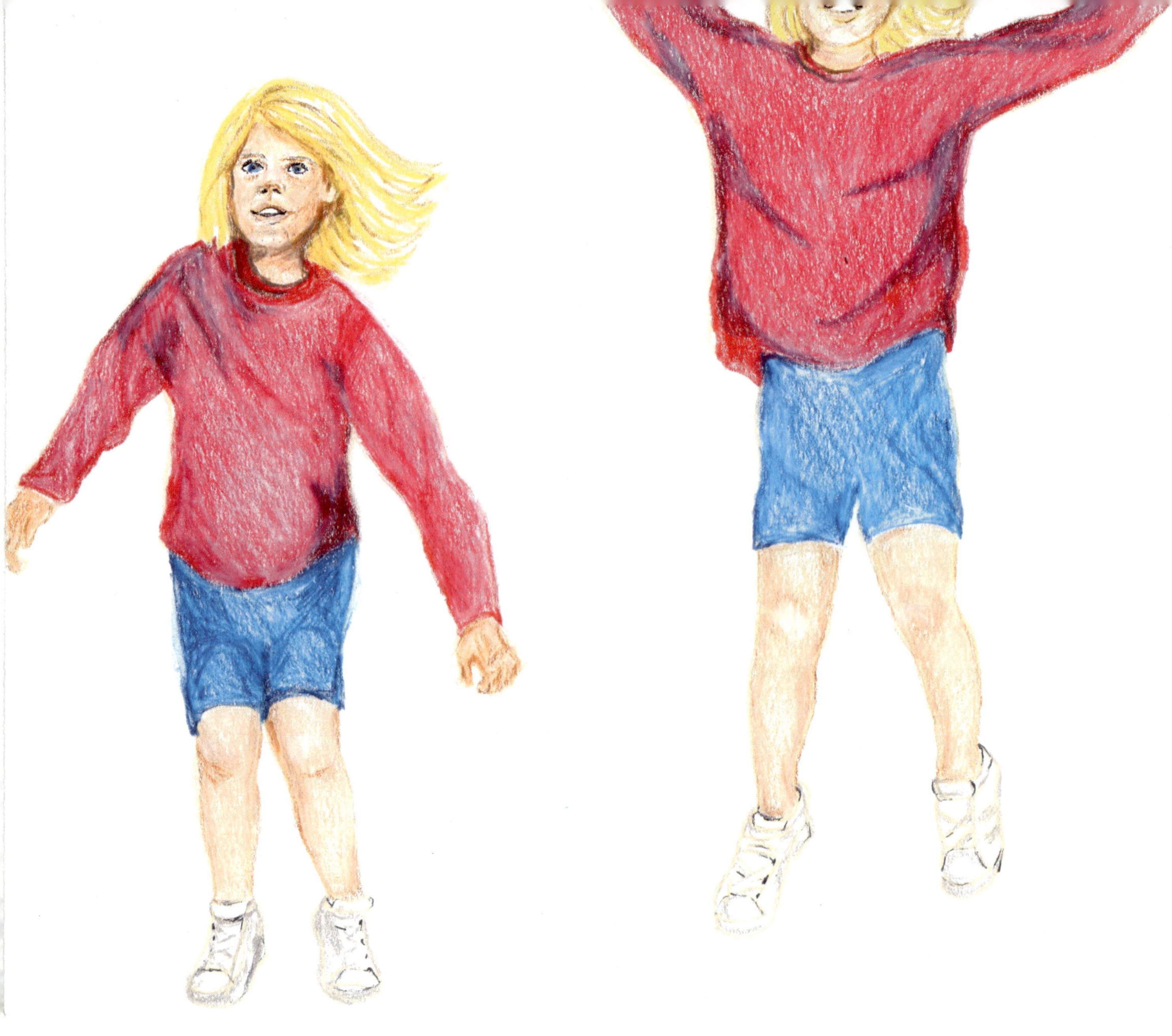

"WHOA! BLUE BETTY!"
 Berkie said with delight.
 "Gliding around your tank so free
your fins are as bright as my blue eyes
I'm so HAPPY you belong to me!"

So on that day, with the sky so BLUE
Betty and Berkie found their match.
A classic DUO, an instant bond,
both shy and brave—forever attached.

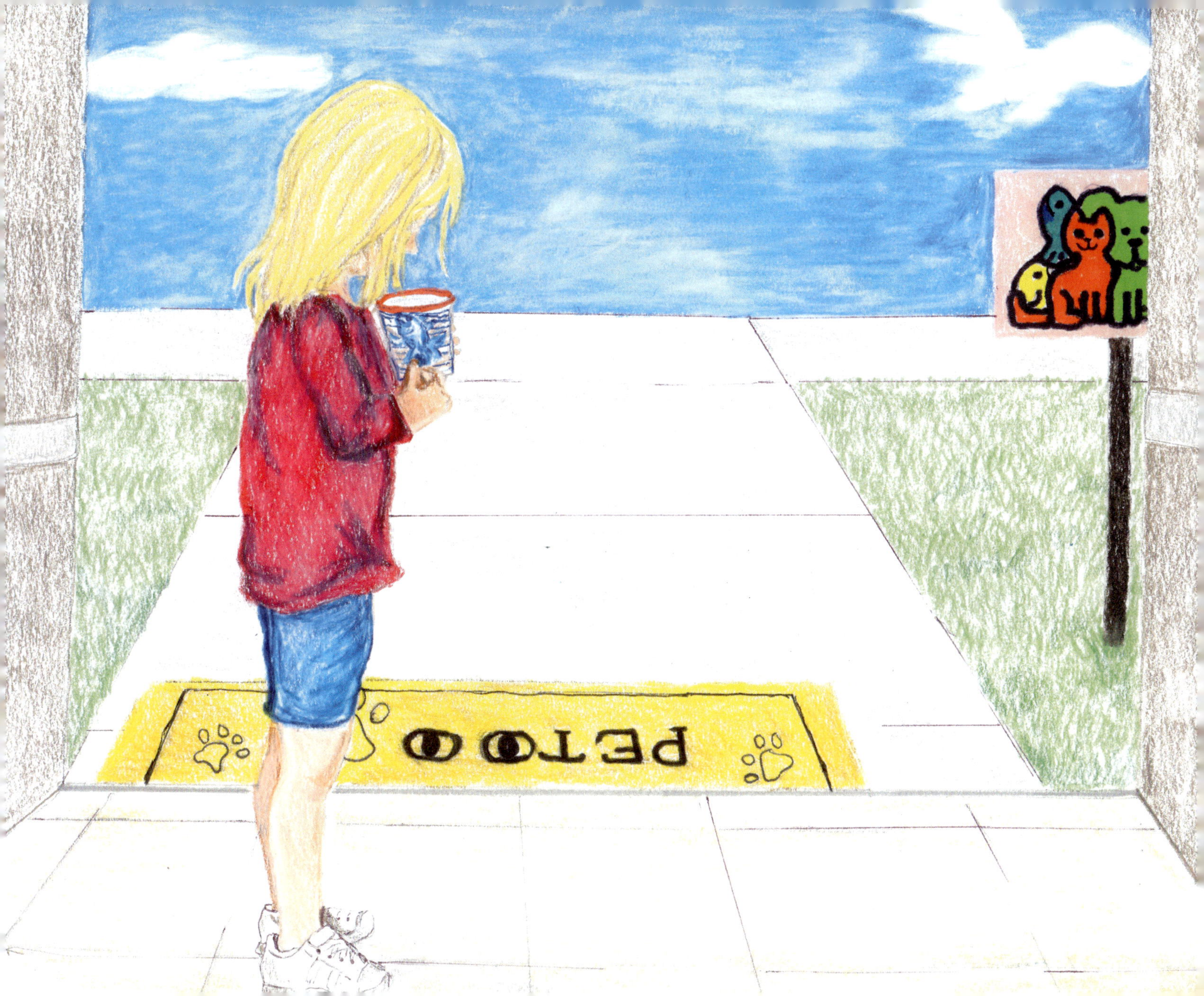
PETCO

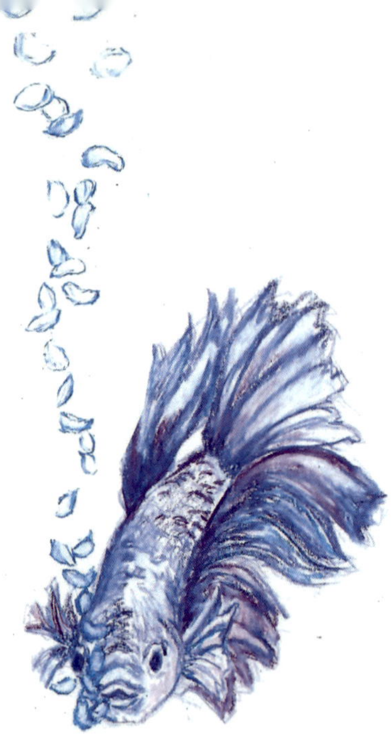